Exotic, Rare, and Fantastical Eggs

*Written and Illustrated
by Jessica Cathryn Feinberg*

With special thanks to:

All fans, friends, and Kickstarter backers whose support made this book possible.

FIRST EDITION
Copyright © 2015 Jessica C. Feinberg
All rights reserved.
ISBN: 978-1-944243-39-5

Contents

Introduction — 4

Identifying Eggs — 5

Earth Eggs — 7

Air Eggs — 20

Fire Eggs — 32

Water Eggs — 46

Metal Eggs — 57

Ice & Snow Eggs — 63

Other Eggs — 66

Index — 73

Introduction

This book is designed to provide a quick pocket sized reference for identifying strange, unusual, and fantastical eggs. Most of the eggs belong to dragons, but additional species such as griffins and phoenixes are also included.

The images of the eggs were mostly illustrated from life (sometimes at great peril), and occasionally for very rare eggs, from a written account. Some variation in egg patterning occurs in nature, but the artist has attempted to ensure that the images herein are as accurate as possible.

The eggs are listed by general type: Earth, Air, Fire, Water, Metal, Ice & Snow, and Other. Within these types the eggs are listed smallest to largest. At the end of the book a full index of all the eggs by name and species is also included.

Please use care and caution when approaching nests, searching for, and handling eggs. The author would hate to be responsible for anyone's untimely demise while hunting for rare eggs.

<u>Identifying Eggs</u>

Identifying the type of a fantastical egg is very important. This will help with proper incubation and hatching. This guide is provided to help with the identification of the strange eggs (or eggshells) you come across. Each egg listing includes the size, clutch size (how many eggs are usually laid), incubation period (if known) and location(s) they are found in.

Where you find an egg can help you identify it, although eggs can become lost and turn up in strange locations. If you find a whole nest of eggs it is generally a good idea to observe it and see if a creature is nearby and taking care of them. The nest itself may also provide clues as to the type of creature it belongs to.

Keep in mind that many eggs, especially dragon eggs, may have very long incubation periods. If you come into possession of an egg that may not hatch in your lifetime please take care to plan for this with an organization or person who can take over care of the egg after your death.

Handling & Transporting Eggs

Always handle eggs carefully as they may be fragile and sensitive to movement. Make sure you have clean, dry hands before picking up an egg. You may find it useful to have gloves or a towel nearby to hold the egg with in case it is difficult to handle (due to the surface texture or temperature).

Temperature and weight may help you determine which section to look under in this book, but remember that eggs may be very hot or cold so check this gingerly with a light touch.

HOT eggs tend to be fire dragons.
COLD eggs tend to be snow and ice dragons.
DAMP or MOIST eggs tend to be water dragons.
HEAVY and/or HARD eggs tend to belong to earth (rock) or metal dragons.

If you find an egg and need to move it, try to preserve the environment as much as possible. For example if you find an egg in a pool of water, make sure you use a bucket of water to move the egg. If the egg is in a freezing location, bring lots of ice to keep it cold and so forth.

EARTH EGGS

Earth creatures include those that dwell in rocks, trees, forests and so forth. Their eggs tend to be muted colors with lots of brown, green, and gray coloration (except for gemstone dragons which have brightly colored eggs).

Some types of earth eggs require sunlight to hatch, while others may need to be in darker locations. Make sure to note the conditions where you find them so you can replicate them at home as needed.

Rough, rock-like eggs usually belong to rock and cavern species. Wooden or nut-shell like eggs belong to forest and tree creatures. Scale-like eggs may belong to earth creatures or, if the egg is hot, you may be better off looking under Fire Eggs.

Glass eggs are VERY fragile and slightly warm to the touch. These belong to "Glass" and "Stained Glass" earth dragons and should be handled with great care.

Myrmecoleon
Formicam leo

Egg Size: 1-2 inches

Incubation: 10 weeks

Clutch Size: 1

Location:
Currently unknown.

Grass Drake
Draco herba

Egg Size: 2 inches

Incubation: 11 weeks

Clutch Size: 4-6

Location:
Hidden hollows in fields of tall grass.

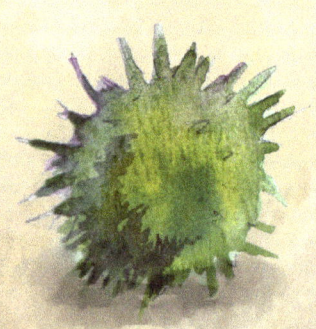

Branch Wyrm
Ramus serpens draco

Egg Size: 2.5 inches

Incubation: 4 months

Clutch Size: 2-3

Location:
Nests built in the in branches of trees. Very well hidden.

Rock Drake
Petram draco

Egg Size: 6-8 inches

Incubation: 3 years

Clutch Size: 1-3

Location:
Nests in rocky hollows close to the surface.

Oak Drake
Quercu petulam dracone

Egg Size: 7-10 inches

Incubation: 8.7 weeks

Clutch Size: 5-7

Location:
Nests near or in oak trees in North America and Europe.

Ruby Dragon
Carbunculus draco

Egg Size: 8 inches

Incubation: 8-14 years

Clutch Size: 1

Location:
Hidden caves in Burma and Greenland near Ruby formations.

Wood Drake
Lingo draco

Egg Size: 8 inches

Incubation: 19 weeks

Clutch Size: 1-3

Location:
Woodland areas near trees. Often mistaken for nuts of some type.

Fungus Drake
Multis fungos draco

Egg Size: 9-12 inches

Incubation: 12 months.

Clutch Size: 2-8

Location:
Eurasian and North American forests. Nests are in moist areas near lots of fungal growth.

Mud Dragon
Draco de lutum

Egg Size: 12 inches

Incubation: 32 months

Clutch Size: 4-6

Location:
Banks of muddy pits in France, Scotland, Canada, and the United States.

Butterfly Drake
Draco de papilionibus

Egg Size: 13 inches

Incubation: 4-6 months

Clutch Size: 2-8

Location:
Well guarded forest nests in Peru and Brazil.

Glass Dragon
Draco vitro luci

Egg Size: 14 inches

Incubation: 19 years

Clutch Size: 1-4

Location:
Near the surface in caves with very hot climates.

Tree Dragon
Arborem major draconis

Egg Size: 16-17 inches

Incubation: 14 months

Clutch Size: 2-6

Location:
In the hollows of very old, large, trees.

Stained Glass Dragon
Draco de coloris vitro

Egg Size: 1.5 feet

Incubation: 28 years

Clutch Size: 1-2

Location:
Large, dimly lit caverns, usually near hot springs.

Cherry Blossom Lung
Prunus serrulata draco

Egg Size: 1.8 feet

Incubation: 2-4 years

Clutch Size: 1

Location:
Surface caves and rocky hollows in Asia (near cherry tree groves).

Jungle Dragon
Truncatis draco

Egg Size: 1-2 feet

Incubation: 2.5 years

Clutch Size: 2-4

Location:
Jungle ruins in the Amazon rainforest.

Moss Dragon
Draco de silva musco

Egg Size: 2 feet

Incubation: 4 years

Clutch Size: 1

Location:
Secluded forests, usually hidden under moss.

Basilisk
Lapidem maledictionem lacerta

Egg Size: 3 feet

Incubation: 75-100 years

Clutch Size: 1-2

Location:
Desert caves and old ruins.

Bengal Hydra
Tigris multa capita draconis

Egg Size: 3.4 feet

Incubation: 5-10 years

Clutch Size: 1

Location:
Well guarded nests, deep in tropical evergreen forests. Very rare.

Bark Drake
Draco cortice

EGG SIZE: 3.5 feet

INCUBATION: 10-12 years

CLUTCH SIZE: 1

LOCATION:
Very rare. Found deep in forests far from human civilization.

Lesser Cave Drake
Minus spelunca draco

EGG SIZE: 3-4 feet

INCUBATION: 12-13 years

CLUTCH SIZE: 1

LOCATION:
Pit-like nests in rocky caverns deep underground.

Forest Hydra
Silva draco multorum capitum

Egg Size: 4-6 feet.

Incubation: Unknown

Clutch Size: 1

Location:
Deep in old, temperate forests.

Sand Wyvern
Harena turbine draconis

Egg Size: 5-8 feet.

Incubation: 100-120 years

Clutch Size: 1

Location:
Hot, dry, desert caves.

EGG GENDER

Usually one cannot determine the gender of a creature from its egg. There are a few exceptions to this, the most notable being the eggs of Glass Dragons. If a glass dragon egg has a distinctly blue or green tint to it there is a 90% chance it is male. If it has a red or pink tent the chances sway towards female.

This is even more noticeable in Stained Glass Dragon eggs. While these eggs are always a variety of colors, female eggs have more warm colors (reds and pinks) and male eggs have cooler colors (blues and greens).

Gendering of other egg types is not exact enough to document yet, but is being studied at IODS.

Air Eggs

Air creature eggs usually weigh less than those belonging to other creatures. They also tend to be more rounded and spotted (much like bird eggs).

Rare to find, luck dragon eggs will be iridescent, smooth, and slightly warm to the touch. They also require an emotionally soothing environment and will not hatch if surrounded by stressful emotions.

Oddly shaped eggs that are very rounded and have swirl patterns are cloud dragon eggs. Lighting dragon eggs are similar, but the patterns are more jagged.

Griffin eggs tend to be very speckled and slightly warmer to the touch than those belonging to air dragons.

Air creature eggs are mostly lighter colors, but there are exceptions (such as some the Lighting Wyvern and the Lupax).

Blue Bee Chaser
Sectator apis draco

Egg Size: 0.3 inches

Incubation: 8-12 weeks

Clutch Size: 3-7

Location:
Nests can be found in late spring. Usually in small trees near gardens or fields of wild flowers.

Lesser Luck Lung
Fortuna draco orientales minor

Egg Size: 2-3 inches

Incubation: 75 years

Clutch Size: 1-2

Location:
Rare and unknown, can sometimes be found in magical black markets.

Domestic Feather Drake
Domesticis draco plumis

Egg Size: 2.5 inches

Incubation: 6 years

Clutch Size: 2-6

Location:
Endangered, only found in conservation programs.

Sunflower Drake
Helianthus draco parvus

Egg Size: 3-4 inches

Incubation: 13 months

Clutch Size: 2-3

Location:
Eggs are hidden among rocks in wildflower fields.

Lavender Luck Dragon
Lavendula fortuna draco

Egg Size: 3.5 inches

Incubation: 8-12 years

Clutch Size: 2-4

Location:
Very old, secluded, groves of fruit trees.

Teal Coatl
Draco hyacintho plumis

Egg Size: 4 inches

Incubation: 6 years

Clutch Size: 2-3

Location:
Nests in tall trees. Look in moist, tropical areas.

__Lamppost Lurker__
Lucerna umbra draco major

EGG SIZE: 4-6 inches

INCUBATION: 4-5 years

CLUTCH SIZE: 2-3

LOCATION:
Secluded cave systems not far from the surface.

__Viper Griffin__
Vipera griffinus

EGG SIZE: 6 inches

INCUBATION: 120 days

CLUTCH SIZE: 1

LOCATION:
Very rare. Only recorded findings were in the Congo, hidden in tall trees.

Lupax
Lupus corvus

EGG SIZE: 8 inches

INCUBATION: Unknown

CLUTCH SIZE: 1

LOCATION:
Very old, large, trees.
Well hidden.

Harpy Griffin
Harpia griffinus

EGG SIZE: 8-10 inches

INCUBATION: 30-40 days

CLUTCH SIZE: 2-3

LOCATION:
Rocky, high mountain,
caves with hidden entrances.

Lightning Drake
Draco fulmini minor

Egg Size: 1 foot

Incubation: 25 years

Clutch Size: 1

Location:
Nests are built in rocky hollows on mountain tops. Look in areas prone to lighting strikes.

Common Griffin
Optimum notum griffinus

Egg Size: 1 foot

Incubation: 40-50 days

Clutch Size: 3

Location:
Caves with narrow entrances. Use caution, griffin nests are heavily guarded.

Peryton
Cervus alatum

EGG SIZE: 1.4 feet

INCUBATION: 3 days

CLUTCH SIZE: 1

LOCATION:
Woodland glades, very rare.

Crested Griffin
Galeae cristasque griffinus

EGG SIZE: 1.5 feet

INCUBATION: 1 year

CLUTCH SIZE: 1-3

LOCATION:
Narrow, well hidden cave openings leading to warm caverns.

Hippogriff
Equum griffinus

Egg Size: 1.8 feet

Incubation: 24-48 hours

Clutch Size: 1

Location:
Nests in grasslands.
Eggs hatch quickly,
but are very rare.

Rainbow Wyvern
Magna draco plumis

Egg Size: 2.3 feet

Incubation: 3 years

Clutch Size: 1

Location:
Tall, sturdy trees in
Coasta Rica rainforests.

Greater Luck Lung
Fortuna draco orientales major

EGG SIZE: 3 feet

INCUBATION: 125 years

CLUTCH SIZE: 1

LOCATION:
Rare, usually hidden in deep mountain caves by the dragon or a society guarding them.

Cloud Lung
Nubibus draconis orientales

EGG SIZE: 3.2 feet

INCUBATION: 42 years

CLUTCH SIZE: 1

LOCATION:
Unknown, but at least one egg exists in the care of WAAPE today.

Lightning Wyvern
Draco fulmini

EGG SIZE: 4 feet

INCUBATION: Unknown

CLUTCH SIZE: 1

LOCATION:
High mountain caves in areas prone to bad weather.

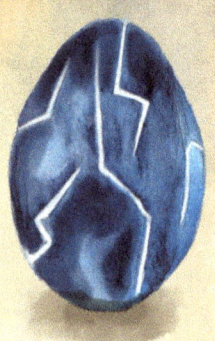

Cloud Hydra
Nubibus draconis multa capita

EGG SIZE: 4 feet

INCUBATION: 120 years

CLUTCH SIZE: 1

LOCATION:
Mountain top nests, but only on mountains tall enough to reach the clouds.

Cloud Drake
Nubibus draconis

Egg Size: 6-10 feet

Incubation: Unknown

Clutch Size: 1

Location: Unknown. Only one has ever been reported.

Roc
Volucris omnis alae gigas

Egg Size: 12-20 feet

Incubation: Unknown

Clutch Size: 1

Location: Remote, sheltered, mountains. Only two ever documented, but no hatching has been observed thus far.

Fire Eggs

The eggs of fire creatures are best detected by their temperature - they tend to be very hot to the touch. They also are usually warmer colors like reds, oranges and yellows, but may occasionally have some purple and black coloration too.

Flame like patterns are a sure sign of a fire creature.

Eggs that resemble lumps of coal or look burned are certainly fire eggs, though they often begin lighter in color and then darken if fire breath is used to keep them warm.

Lava and Magma Dragon eggs have brightly colored veining patterns on them in reds and yellows. These eggs are VERY HOT and should not be picked up without proper precautions.

Char Toad
Ambustam Draco

Egg Size: 1/3 inch

Incubation: 72 hours

Clutch Size: 2-4

Location:
Nests in rocky areas
rich with iron deposits

Matchstick Drake
Draco ignis accendens

Egg Size: 1/2 inch

Incubation: 10 days

Clutch Size: 3-7

Location:
In forgotten basements or
very dry attics during
the hottest summer months.

Charcoal Drake
Sicut carbones draco

Egg Size: 1/2 inch

Incubation: 2 months

Clutch Size: 4-6

Location:
Caves near fires or charcoal pits.

Spark Lung
Ignis manducans draconis

Egg Size: 1/2 inch

Incubation: 10 years

Clutch Size: 4

Location:
China, Japan, and Korea. Nests in abandoned buildings in dark corners.

Blue Phoenix
Avis ignis renascentia hyacinthinas

EGG SIZE: 1 inch

INCUBATION: Unknown

CLUTCH SIZE: 1-3

LOCATION:
Unknown. Blue Phoenixes are very rare. Little is known about them. Egg is illustrated based on old historical records at FLAME.

Fire Lizard
Lacerta ignis spiritus

EGG SIZE: 1.2 inches

INCUBATION: 8 days

CLUTCH SIZE: 4-10

LOCATION:
Eggs laid in hottest summer months. Look for rocky hollows and holes. Common in the Southwestern United States and Northwestern Mexico.

Greater Fire Lung
Ignem respiratio draconis

Egg Size: 1-2 inches

Incubation: 18 months

Clutch Size: 1-5

Location:
Small, well hidden, caves in China and Japan.

Dark Phoenix
Avis ignis (tenebris plumis)

Egg Size: 1-2 inches

Incubation: 12 weeks

Clutch Size: 1

Location:
Nests in very old forests, especially those that have had recent lighting strikes.

Magma Drake
Ardens petram draco

EGG SIZE: 2 inches

INCUBATION: Unknown

CLUTCH SIZE: Unknown

LOCATION:
Near volcanic activity.

CAUTION: Do not pick up. Causes burns that never fully heal.

Domestic Phoenix
Avis ignis renascentia domesticatis

EGG SIZE: 2-3 inches

INCUBATION: 12 weeks

CLUTCH SIZE: 1

LOCATION:
As these are domesticated it will lay eggs wherever nesting space is provided.

Egyptian Phoenix
Aegyptius avis ignis renascentia

Egg Size: 3 inches

Incubation: 21 months

Clutch Size: 1

Location:
Secluded, sheltered, nests near water in Egypt.

Blue Flame Drake
Hyacinthinas ignis draco

Egg Size: 3-5 inches

Incubation: 48 hours

Clutch Size: 1

Location:
High trees in Costa Rica.

Russian Firebird
Fortuna avis flammarum

Egg Size: 4.5 inches

Incubation: 28-30 days

Clutch Size: 4-6

Location:
During the warmer months look for nests in trees or on rocky ledges near Firebird sightings.

Sun Wyvern
Pennata solis draco

Egg Size: 5 inches

Incubation: 4 months

Clutch Size: 1

Location:
Very large trees in tropical climates.

Wild Phoenix
Avis ignis renascentia

Egg Size: 4-6 inches

Incubation: 12-14 weeks

Clutch Size: 1

Location:
Secluded rocky hollows on high cliffs or very old trees. Rare to find.

Basan
Ignum spirans pullum

Egg Size: 8 inches

Incubation: 3 weeks

Clutch Size: 1-5

Location:
Bamboo groves in the mountains of Japan. Look for very, very large, chicken-like eggs with swirl patterns.

Redwood Dragons
Sequoiadendron giganteum draco

EGG SIZE: 10-14 inches

INCUBATION: 6 months

CLUTCH SIZE: 1

LOCATION:
Redwood forests in the hollows of trees.

Persian Phoenix
Persica avis ignis renascentia

EGG SIZE: 1-1.5 feet

INCUBATION: 7-10 days

CLUTCH SIZE: 1-3

LOCATION:
Lays eggs every 100-250 years in shallow cave-like hollows that help shelter the nest.

Fire Salamander
Ignus Salamandra

Egg Size: 1-15 inches

Incubation: 2-3 weeks

Clutch Size: 1-5

Location:
Moist, rocky caves.

Common Fire Drake
Ignis draco

Egg Size: 24-32 inches

Incubation: 20-24 months

Clutch Size: 3-8

Location:
Caverns in Asia
and parts of Europe.

FIRE SALAMANDER COLORATION

As with Salamanders themselves, Salamander eggs may vary greatly in both size and color. The red and yellow eggs are usually laid by those living near salty brine pools. Blue and green eggs are laid by those near copper deposits.

When hatched, the Salamander may have more of the coloration of the egg it came from, but over time its color may shift depending on diet and environment.

Fire Hydra
Multiceps ignis draconi

Egg Size: 3.2 feet

Incubation: 50-60 years

Clutch Size: 1

Location:
Deep mountain caves.

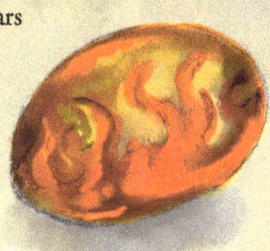

Russian Hydra
Viridis multa capita draconis

Egg Size: 4-5 feet

Incubation: 100-130 years

Clutch Size: 1

Location:
Deep cave systems in Russia.

Lava Drake
Solumque est draco

EGG SIZE: 1 yard

INCUBATION: 300 years

CLUTCH SIZE: 1

LOCATION:
Very hot caves with volcanic activity.

Lava Lord
Draco ardentis solumque

EGG SIZE: Estimated as massive

INCUBATION: Unknown

CLUTCH SIZE: Unknown

LOCATION:
Volcanos. Due to volcanic activity details are unknown.

WATER EGGS

Water creatures may dwell full time in lakes, oceans, seas, rivers or streams. They may also be amphibians - spending time both in and out of the water.

Slimy, moist eggs belong to swamp and marsh dragons.

Large, blue-green eggs found on the bottom of lakes and oceans usually belong to lake or sea serpents. They tend to have very protective parents and should not be disturbed.

Eggs found in water may be sensitive to drying out. Other factors about the such as temperature, salt and mineral content, of the water should be considered. If you plan to move an egg found in water use great care and plan to move it with a good deal of the water you found it in (using a bucket or tank). Be sure to note if you found the egg in salt or freshwater and keep it in the same type of water until it hatches.

Lillypad Draconis
Nymphaeaceae draco

EGG SIZE: 1/4 inch

INCUBATION: 48 hours

CLUTCH SIZE: 8-20

LOCATION:
Eggs are laid and hatched underwater in small ponds or streams.

Sink Serpent
Serpens lava pelvim

EGG SIZE: 1/3 inch

INCUBATION: 4 years

CLUTCH SIZE: 3-8

LOCATION:
If domestic will need a safe private part of their tank or habitat. In the wild they find rocky pools away from other animals and people.

Domestic Water Dragon
Aureum draconem pisces

Egg Size: 1/2 inch

Incubation: 4-7 days

Clutch Size: 3-5

Location:
Eggs are usually only to be found with dragon breeders as this is a domesticated species.

Minor Water Dragon
Minima aquous draconis

Egg Size: 1/2 inch

Incubation: 48 hours

Clutch Size: 1

Location:
Rocky underwater areas with lots of plant growth for camouflage.

Frilled Sea Drake
Spina Pterois Draco

Egg Size: 1 inch

Incubation: 48 hours

Clutch Size: 2-6

Location:
Small underwater caves and sheltered rock hollows in the Pacific Ocean.

Gold Scaled Water Drake
Aurum escensu aqua draco

Egg Size: 1.3 inches

Incubation: 4-5 months

Clutch Size: 3-8

Location:
Fresh water caverns including underground lakes and rivers.

River Drake
Draconem fluminis

Egg Size: 1.3 inches

Incubation: 6 weeks

Clutch Size: 1

Location:
North Pacific ocean during spawning season.

Rainbow Drake
Arcus pluvius aquas draco

Egg Size: 1.4 inches

Incubation: 6 weeks

Clutch Size: 1

Location:
Small bodies of water in Africa. The domesticated variety can be found in rare exotic pet stores if you know who to ask.

Seahorse Drake
Hippocampus draco

EGG SIZE: 2-5 inches

INCUBATION: 4 months

CLUTCH SIZE: 6-20

LOCATION:
Near coral reefs, often hidden safely among the coral where they are mistaken for some sort of fish egg.

Seashell Drake
Draco conchis marinis

EGG SIZE: 3 Inches

INCUBATION: __

CLUTCH SIZE: __

LOCATION:
On beaches safely away from the water. Resembles a seashell, but is warm to the touch and much heavier.

Dragon Seal
Phoca draco

EGG SIZE: 3.5 inches

INCUBATION: 2 weeks

CLUTCH SIZE: 1

LOCATION: Secluded beaches in tropical climates.

Tidal Drake
Draco maritimos aestus maximos

EGG SIZE: 3-4 inches

INCUBATION: 18 months

CLUTCH SIZE: 1

LOCATION: Their eggs resemble a shell or rock with swirly patterns and can be found near or in tide pools.

Kappa
Puer autem fluminis

EGG SIZE: 5 inches

INCUBATION: 24 hours

CLUTCH SIZE: 3-6

LOCATION:
River banks in sand, usually under the full moon.

Lesser Marsh Wyrm
Draconem serpentem paludis

EGG SIZE: 8 inches

INCUBATION: 8 months

CLUTCH SIZE: 7-10

LOCATION:
Muddy caves on the banks of marshes and swamps.

Lake Serpent
Serpens ex lacu

EGG SIZE: 2-5 feet

INCUBATION: 60 years

CLUTCH SIZE: 1

LOCATION:
Underwater caverns connected to lakes.

Swamp Dragon
Draco paludem

EGG SIZE: 4-5 feet

INCUBATION: 25-30 years

CLUTCH SIZE: 1-2

LOCATION:
Hidden under moss and other plant life in swamps.

Greater Reef Dragon
Magnus alcyoneum petra draco

EGG SIZE: 6-10 feet

INCUBATION: 95 years

CLUTCH SIZE: 1

LOCATION:
Near coral reefs, usually hidden in old shipwrecks.

Coral Reef Serpent
Alcyoneum scopulos serpentem

EGG SIZE: 8.4 feet

INCUBATION: 3 years

CLUTCH SIZE: 1-4

LOCATION:
Very, very rare. Only laid once every 100 years in hard to access parts of the reef and are fiercely protected.

Rainbow Serpent
Arcus pluvius aquas serpentis

Egg Size: 8-12 feet

Incubation: Unknown

Clutch Size: 1-3

Location:
Large caves near rivers in Australia and Polynesia.

Sea Serpent
Serpentis Maris

Egg Size: 10-12 feet

Incubation: Unknown

Clutch Size: 1

Location:
Several have been observed in underwater caverns deep in the sea. To date none have hatched so incubation time is not known.

METAL EGGS

Metal eggs are easy to identify, but very rare to find. They have metallic colors and textures. They also tend to be heavier than many other types of eggs.

Depending on the creature, the egg may be manufactured or laid or have some magical component. Clockwork eggs are really easy to identify but are very fragile and may need special care such as winding or oiling.

Many times metal eggs are mistaken for antiques, trinkets and keepsakes. As many take over a hundred years to hatch, people often don't realize they are in possession of an egg at all. Some myths say metal creature eggs have magical powers, or are simply desired for their worth. Stories like Jack and the Beanstalk feature golden eggs, though the original version had a dragon and not a goose.

Lead Drake
Plumbum draco

Egg Size: 1/2 inch

Incubation: 3 years

Clutch Size: 3-8

Location:
These small, VERY heavy eggs are often mistaken for marbles or ball bearings. They just seem to turn up in random places.

Gold Leaf Drake
Aurum folium draco

Egg Size: 1.6 inches

Incubation: 2 years

Clutch Size: 1

Location:
Caves in Germany and some parts of the United States. Also frequently traded on the black market.

Golden Sword Drake
Aurum gladiis draco custos

EGG SIZE: 2-3 inches

INCUBATION: 18 months

CLUTCH SIZE: 1-5

LOCATION:
Breeders of magical creatures sometimes have access to these eggs. They may also be found in old ruins and caves.

Titanium Drake
Multos colores titanium draco

EGG SIZE: 4 inches

INCUBATION: 18 months

CLUTCH SIZE: 1

LOCATION:
Great Britain, especially near Cornwall. Look for small caves near fresh water.

Clockwork Drake

Egg Size: 4 inches

Incubation: Varies

Clutch Size: 1

Location:
Must be created, usually by a combination of enchantment and clockwork mechanics. Sometimes sold by witches and sorcerers.

Metal Avian Egg

Egg Size: 5 inches

Incubation: Unknown

Clutch Size: Unknown

Location:
A number of these eggs are currently in circulation on the black market. Supposedly they contain some form of metal or clockwork bird, but none have hatched yet so they may just be a hoax.

Clockwork Wyvern

Egg Size: 1.5 feet

Incubation: Varies

Clutch Size: Varies

Location:
Mystical antique stores, eccentric wizard's libraries, and other such random locals.

Silver Dragon
Argentum draco

Egg Size: 2 feet

Incubation: 100 years

Clutch Size: 1-2

Location:
Nests in caves in mountains throughout Northern Europe.

Clockwork Hydra

Egg Size: 2.6 feet

Incubation: Random

Clutch Size: 1

Location:
Deep cave systems in Turkey and a few museums and private collectors are known to have them.

Greater Gold Dragon
Magnus aurum draco

Egg Size: 8 feet

Incubation: 140 years

Clutch Size: 1-3

Location:
Nests are well hidden in deep cave systems throughout Europe.

Ice & Snow Eggs

Ice and snow eggs are found in colder climates and are usually very cold to the touch. Many appear ice-like or are buried in snow to deter predators.

Note that these eggs may be fragile and sensitive to temperature changes. Handle them gently, using gloves. Always note the temperature you find these eggs at and try to maintain it until they hatch.

Ice Cube Snatcher
Glacies cubum furem

Egg Size: 1/4 inch

Incubation: 24 hours

Clutch Size: 2-12

Location:
Walk in freezers, igloos, snow forts, small icy caves.

Frost Drake
Draco pruina

Egg Size: 3-4 inches

Incubation: 2 months

Clutch Size: 2-8

Location:
Icy caves in colder climates. Eggs must be kept below freezing for the incubation period.

Black Ice Drake
Nigrum draco glacies

Egg Size: 7-10 inches

Incubation: 9 months

Clutch Size: 1-3

Location:
Very dark, cold caves. Always laid during the coldest winter months. Fairly rare.

Snow Drake
Minor draco nix

Egg Size: 8 inches

Incubation: 2 years

Clutch Size: 1

Location:
High caves on snowy mountain tops

Iceberg Draconis
Insulam glacies draco

Egg Size: Massive

Incubation: Unknown

Clutch Size: 1

Location:
Appears as small, rounded, icebergs floating near glaciers.

OTHER EGGS

The eggs in this section belong to creatures that really don't fit into a specific element or natural environment. These are creatures that have evolved to integrate themselves into human environments such as bookstores, libraries, and junk yards.

Identifying some of these eggs can be tricky (except for book wyrms and literary dragons who always wrap their eggs in paper), and there are still many new varieties being discovered and documented.

Ink Gremlin
Draco de atramento vertuntur

Egg Size: 1/4 inch

Incubation: 48 days

Clutch Size: 4-12

Location:
Desk drawers, under cabinets, and any other dark locations near offices and art studios. Eggs are often mistaken for rocks or small ball bearings.

Blue Banded Pen Snatcher
Calamum rapientem

Egg Size: 1/2 inch

Incubation: 3 days

Clutch Size: 1

Location:
Desk drawers, office supply warehouses, and dusty forgotten storage closets.

Coffee Drake
Capulus dracone

Egg Size: 3/4 inch

Incubation: 48 hours

Clutch Size: 1-10

Location:
Generally near sources of caffeine such as coffee bean suppliers, coffee shop pantries, and so forth.

Noodle Snatcher
Draco rapientem pasta

Egg Size: 3/4 inch

Incubation: 4 days

Clutch Size: 2-8

Location:
Near a large supply of food, noodles of some kind if possible. Check pantries, closets and alley-ways near pasta-serving restaurants.

Venomous Drake
Draco venenatorum

EGG SIZE: 1 inch

INCUBATION: 9 weeks

CLUTCH SIZE: 1

LOCATION:
Unknown, those who have come into contact with these eggs usually suffer from poisoning. Avoid at all costs.

Lesser Library Drake
Bibliomanias draconis

EGG SIZE: 2.5 inches

INCUBATION: 7-8 months

CLUTCH SIZE: 1-3

LOCATION:
Forgotten parts of libraries and antiquarian booksellers.

Gold Tome Guardian
Draco qui custodit libros

Egg Size: 3 inches

Incubation: 6 months

Clutch Size: 1

Location: Dusty library cellars, forgotten ruins, and museum basements.

Skull Snatcher
Calvariam rapientem

Egg Size: 3-4 inches

Incubation: 2-4 weeks

Clutch Size: 3-12

Location: Graveyards and sites with lots of old bones or fossils.

Greater Library Drake
Draco de bibliotheca

EGG SIZE: 12-14 inches

INCUBATION: 3 years

CLUTCH SIZE: 1

LOCATION:
Usually kept safe by the parent or a bookstore owner or librarian.

Yellow-Breasted Sock Snatcher
Draco soccum abrepta

EGG SIZE: 12-15 inches

INCUBATION: 7 months

CLUTCH SIZE: 3-9

LOCATION:
Messy closets and boxes of clothing in basements or attics.

Literary Dragon
Magna draco de libris

Egg Size: 2-3 feet

Incubation: Unknown

Clutch Size: 1

Location:
Very rare. One is known to be in the care of the Grand Clockwork Library.

Bugger
Vehiculo perticam

Egg Size: 3.2 feet

Incubation: 18-20 months

Clutch Size: 1

Location:
Junk and scrap yards, usually in strange nests built out of old cars and scrap metal.

Index

Bark Drake, 17
Basan, 40
Basilisk, 16
Bengal Hydra, 16
Black Ice Drake, 64
Blue Banded Pen Snatcher, 67
Blue Bee Chaser, 21
Blue Flame Drake, 38
Blue Phoenix, 35
Branch Wyrm, 9
Bugger, 72
Butterfly Drake, 12
Charcoal Drake, 34
Char Toad, 33
Cherry Blossom Lung, 14
Clockwork Drake, 60
Clockwork Hydra, 62
Clockwork Wyvern, 61
Cloud Drake, 31
Cloud Hydra, 30
Cloud Lung, 29
Coffee Drake, 68
Common Fire Drake, 42
Common Griffin, 26
Coral Reef Serpent, 55
Crested Griffin, 27
Dark Phoenix, 36
Domestic Feather Drake, 22
Domestic Phoenix, 37
Domestic Water Dragon, 48
Dragon Seal, 52
Egyptian Phoenix, 38
Fire Hydra, 44
Fire Lizard, 35
Fire Salamander, 42

Forest Hydra, 18
Frilled Sea Drake, 49
Frost Drake, 64
Fungus Drake, 11
Glass Dragon, 13
Golden Sword Drake, 59
Gold Leaf Drake, 58
Gold Scaled Water Drake, 49
Gold Tome Guardian, 70
Grass Drake, 8
Greater Fire Lung, 36
Greater Gold Dragon, 62
Greater Library Drake, 71
Greater Luck Lung, 29
Greater Reef Dragon, 55
Harpy Griffin, 25
Hippogriff, 28
Iceberg Draconis, 65
Ice Cube Snatcher, 63
Ink Gremlin, 67
Jungle Dragon, 15
Kappa, 53
Lake Serpent, 54
Lamppost Lurker, 24
Lava Drake, 45
Lava Lord, 45
Lavender Luck Dragon, 23
Lead Drake, 58
Lesser Cave Drake, 17
Lesser Library Drake, 69
Lesser Luck Lung, 21
Lesser Marsh Wyrm, 53
Lightning Drake, 26
Lightning Wyvern, 30
Lillypad Draconis, 47

Literary Dragon, 72
Lupax, 25
Magma Drake, 37
Matchstick Drake, 33
Metal Avian Egg, 60
Minor Water Dragon, 48
Moss Dragon, 15
Mud Dragon, 12
Myrmecoleon, 8
Noodle Snatcher, 68
Oak Drake, 10
Persian Phoenix, 41
Peryton, 27
Rainbow Drake, 50
Rainbow Serpent, 56
Rainbow Wyvern, 28
Redwood Dragons, 41
River Drake, 50
Roc, 31
Rock Drake, 9
Ruby Dragon, 10
Russian Firebird, 39
Russian Hydra, 44
Sand Wyvern, 18
Seahorse Drake, 51
Sea Serpent, 56
Seashell Drake, 51
Silver Dragon, 61
Sink Serpent, 47
Skull Snatcher, 70
Snow Drake, 65
Sock Snatcher, 71
Spark Lung, 34
Stained Glass Dragon, 14
Sunflower Drake, 22
Sun Wyvern, 39
Swamp Dragon, 54
Teal Coatl, 23
Tidal Drake, 52
Titanium Drake, 59
Tree Dragon, 13
Venomous Drake, 69
Viper Griffin, 24
Wild Phoenix, 40
Wood Drake, 11

LUNGS
Cherry Blossom Lung, 14
Cloud Lung, 29
Greater Fire Lung, 36
Greater Luck Lung, 29
Lesser Luck Lung, 21
Spark Lung, 34

HYDRAS
Bengal Hydra, 16
Clockwork Hydra, 62
Cloud Hydra, 30
Fire Hydra, 44
Forest Hydra, 18
Russian Hydra, 44

SERPENTS & WYRMS
Branch Wyrm, 9
Coral Reef Serpent, 55
Lake Serpent, 54
Lesser Marsh Wyrm, 53
Rainbow Serpent, 56
Sea Serpent, 56
Sink Serpent, 47

DRAKES
Bark Drake, 17
Black Ice Drake, 64
Blue Flame Drake, 38
Butterfly Drake, 12
Charcoal Drake, 34
Clockwork Drake, 60
Cloud Drake, 31
Coffee Drake, 68
Common Fire Drake, 42
Domestic Feather Drake, 22
Frilled Sea Drake, 49
Frost Drake, 64
Fungus Drake, 11
Golden Sword Drake, 59
Gold Leaf Drake, 58
Gold Scaled Water Drake, 49
Grass Drake, 8
Greater Library Drake, 71
Lava Drake, 45
Lead Drake, 58
Lesser Cave Drake, 17
Lesser Library Drake, 69
Lightning Drake, 26
Magma Drake, 37
Matchstick Drake, 33
Oak Drake, 10
Rainbow Drake, 50
River Drake, 50
Rock Drake, 9
Seahorse Drake, 51
Seashell Drake, 51
Snow Drake, 65
Sunflower Drake, 22
Tidal Drake, 52
Titanium Drake, 59
Venomous Drake, 69
Wood Drake, 11

WYVERNS
Clockwork Wyvern, 61
Lightning Wyvern, 30
Rainbow Wyvern, 28
Sand Wyvern, 18
Sun Wyvern, 39
Teal Coatl, 23

PHOENIXES
Blue Phoenix, 35
Dark Phoenix, 36
Domestic Phoenix, 37
Egyptian Phoenix, 38
Persian Phoenix, 41
Wild Phoenix, 40

HYBRIDS
Common Griffin, 26
Crested Griffin, 27
Harpy Griffin, 25
Hippogriff, 28
Lupax, 25
Myrmecoleon, 8
Peryton, 27
Viper Griffin, 24

About the Author

Jessica Cathryn Feinberg is a driven, quirky, creative gal who resides in Tucson, Arizona with a house full of books, cats, dragons, and art supplies.

Jessica has been fascinated by goblins and other fae since she was very young and has dedicated her life to writing, drawing, painting, and following in the footsteps of mysterious creatures.

She is best known for her dragon, clockwork, and wildlife artwork as well as her field guides to rare creatures.

You can meet Jessica at many southwest events! For more information visit Artlair.com

www.ingramcontent.com/pod-product-compliance
Ingram Content Group UK Ltd.
Pitfield, Milton Keynes, MK11 3LW, UK
UKHW020246240426
12048UKWH00027B/163